To clever Adeline, Amelia, & Ava~

GO BOLDLY...
with books!

Lisl H. D. 2019.

# If You Had a Jetpack...

Words by
**LISL H. DETLEFSEN**

Illustrated by
**LINZIE HUNTER**

where would YOU go?

Alfred A. Knopf · New York

If you found yourself bored, with nothing to do,
you could build your own

JETPACK.

Putting it together might be tricky.

But since you're clever,

you'd figure it out.

Eventually.

While learning how to fly, your little
brother would see you and get jealous.
So you'd have to build him a jetpack, too.

And teach him how to use it.

PATIENTLY.

Once you both got the hang of it, you'd want to show your jetpacks to all of your friends at school.

GO

RIGHT

LEFT

JETPACK

You could demonstrate how it works during **SHOW** and **SHARE** time.

Cruise through the cafeteria line at lunch.

And play TURBO TAG at recess.

CAUTIOUSLY.

After soaring around school all day, you might get called down to the office.

OOOFF!

The principal would explain that his car has a flat tire...

and ask you for a ride home.

Politely.

Your mom would be so proud of you for helping
the principal that she'd be in an extra-good mood.
You'd decide it was the perfect time to ask if you
could fly south to visit your **Nana.**

Naturally, your little brother would beg to come along.

PLEASE!

TAKE Me!

Persistently.

Your mom would agree, but not before making you both pinkie-promise to be careful.

And wear your helmets.

And call when you get there.

But after all that, you'd be cleared for takeoff!

Immediately.

After seeing you fly into her yard, Nana would probably ask to borrow your jetpack.

Convincing her to give it
back would be difficult,

so you might
have to insist.

Firmly.

You could thank Nana for returning your jetpack by helping her with a few errands.

You'd shop for her groceries.

And take her pet for a walk.

AND pick up her new golf clubs.

While delivering Nana's dry cleaning, you might be reminded that you've always wanted to visit the

**ASTRONAUTS**

in space.

So you'd say good-bye to Nana and your little brother and prepare for *departure!*

# BOLDLY!

When you arrived at the SPACE STATION,
the astronauts would be so blown away
by your clever homemade JETPACK
that they'd invite you to hang out for a while.

The astronauts would be so impressed that they'd call the PRESIDENT to let her know. The president would want to honor your service with a special medal.

The award ceremony would be all over the news!

There would be photographs to take, interviews to give, and autographs to sign.

(Modestly.)

After all that attention,
you might need a little break.

So you'd fly away to <u>relax</u>
on the sandy beach of a deserted planet.

Or perhaps you'd head someplace where you'd blend in with the crowd.

Unexpectedly.

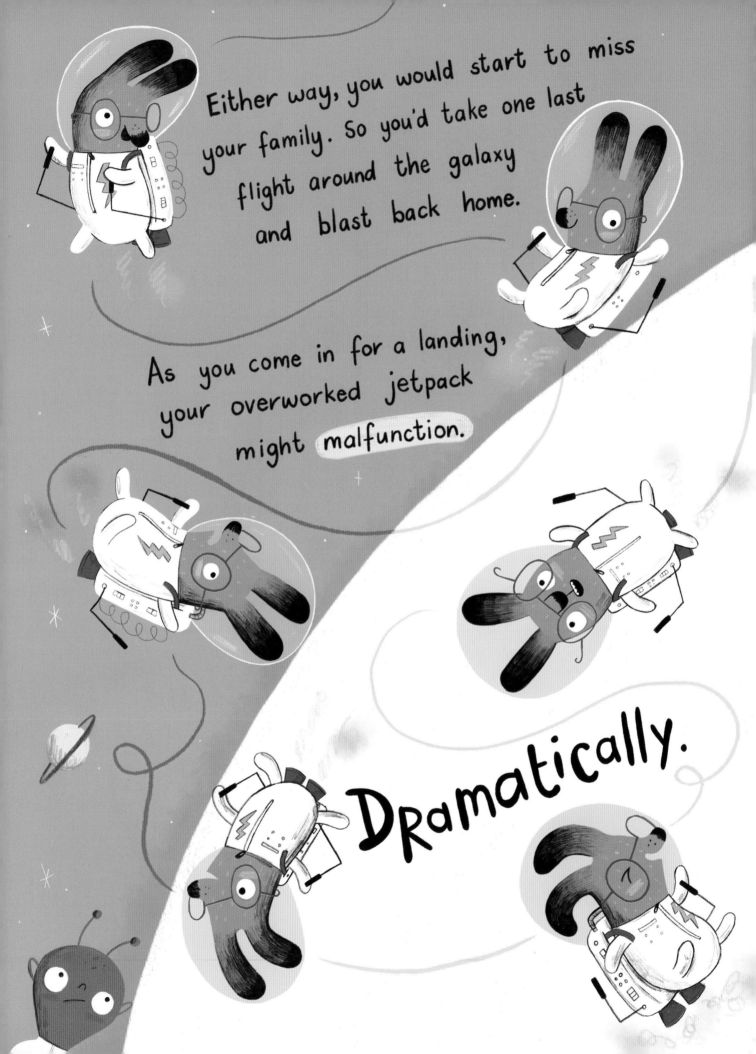

Either way, you would start to miss your family. So you'd take one last flight around the galaxy and blast back home.

As you come in for a landing, your overworked jetpack might malfunction.

Dramatically.

Luckily, your mom would be so HAPPY to see her favorite jetpacker that she wouldn't scold you for making such a **Big Mess.**

But she would want to go back to Nana's house to pick up your little brother.

And since your **JET**PACK needs repairs, you'd have to take a BORING car ride to get there.

Of course, you're never BoRed for very long.

After all, a clever person like you can do ANYTHING.

THIS IS A BORZOI BOOK PUBLISHED BY ALFRED A. KNOPF

Text copyright © 2018 by Lisl H. Detlefsen

Jacket art and interior illustrations copyright © 2018 by Linzie Hunter

All rights reserved. Published in the United States by Alfred A. Knopf,

an imprint of Random House Children's Books, a division of Penguin Random House LLC, New York.

Knopf, Borzoi Books, and the colophon are registered trademarks of Penguin Random House LLC.

Visit us on the Web! rhcbooks.com

Educators and librarians, for a variety of teaching tools, visit us at RHTeachersLibrarians.com

*Library of Congress Cataloging-in-Publication Data*

Names: Detlefsen, Lisl H., author. | Hunter, Linzie, illustrator.

Title: If you had a jetpack / by Lisl Detlefsen ; illustrated by Linzie Hunter.

Description: First edition. | New York : Alfred A. Knopf, 2018. | Summary: Invites the reader to imagine what it would be like

to build and use a jetpack at home, at school, and even on a long voyage or two.

Identifiers: LCCN 2016030610 (print) | LCCN 2016058138 (ebook) | ISBN 978-0-399-55329-5 (trade) |

ISBN 978-0-399-55330-1 (lib. bdg.) | ISBN 978-0-399-55331-8 (ebook)

Subjects: | CYAC: Imagination—Fiction. | Flight—Fiction.

Classification: LCC PZ7.1.D478 If 2018 (print) | LCC PZ7.1.D478 (ebook) | DDC [E]—dc23

The illustrations were created using Procreate on iPad pro and Photoshop.

MANUFACTURED IN CHINA

April 2018      10 9 8 7 6 5 4 3 2      First Edition

Random House Children's Books supports the First Amendment and celebrates the right to read.